W9-AJT-308

Date: 02/01/12

J 599.799 RAK
Rake, Jody Sullivan.
Walruses /

Under the Sea
Walruses

by Jody Sullivan Rake

Consulting Editor: Gail Saunders-Smith, PhD

Consultant: Debbie Nuzzolo, Education Manager
SeaWorld, San Diego, California

Capstone
press®

Mankato, Minnesota

Pebble Plus is published by Capstone Press,
151 Good Counsel Drive, P.O. Box 669, Mankato, Minnesota 56002.
www.capstonepress.com

1 2 3 4 5 6 12 11 10 09 08 07

Library of Congress Cataloging-in-Publication Data
Rake, Jody Sullivan.
    Walruses / by Jody Sullivan Rake.
    p. cm.—(Pebble Plus. Under the sea)
    Summary: "Simple text and photographs present walruses and their lives under the sea"—Provided by
publisher.
    Includes bibliographical references and index.
    ISBN-13: 978-0-7368-6726-9 (hardcover)
    ISBN-10: 0-7368-6726-0 (hardcover)
    1. Walrus—Juvenile literature. I. Title. II. Series.
QL737.P62R35 2007
599.79'9—dc22   2006020380

Editorial Credits
Martha E. H. Rustad, editor; Juliette Peters, set designer; Patrick Dentinger, book designer;
    Wanda Winch, photo researcher/photo editor

Photo Credits
Kevin Schafer Photography, 1
Minden Pictures/Foto Natura/Rinie Van Meurs, 6–7
Nature Picture Library/Doc White, 4–5
Peter Arnold/Kelvin Aitken, 8–9; Steven Kazlowski, 20–21
SeaPics.com/Doc White, 16–17; Goran Ehlme, 18–19; Steven Kazlowski, cover, 10–11
Tom & Pat Leeson, 12–13, 14–15

Note to Parents and Teachers

The Under the Sea set supports national science standards related to the diversity and unity of life. This book describes and illustrates walruses. The images support early readers in understanding the text. The repetition of words and phrases helps early readers learn new words. This book also introduces early readers to subject-specific vocabulary words, which are defined in the Glossary section. Early readers may need assistance to read some words and to use the Table of Contents, Glossary, Read More, Internet Sites, and Index sections of the book.

Table of Contents

What Are Walruses?

Walruses are mammals
that live in herds.
They live on ice and land.
They swim in the cold sea.

Walruses are very big.
They can be the size
of a small car.

Body Parts

Walruses have fat
called blubber.
Blubber and thick skin
keep them warm.

Walruses have
two long tusks.
Tusks help walruses pull
themselves out of the water.

Walruses have four flippers.

Walruses flap their back

flippers to swim.

What Walruses Do

Walruses use their front
and back flippers to walk
on land and ice.

Walruses swim
in the sea
to find food.

Walruses feel
along the sea floor
with their many whiskers.
They eat the shellfish
they find.

Under the Sea

Walruses walk on the ice
and swim under the cold sea.

Glossary

flipper—a flat limb with bones on the bodies of some animals; walruses use their flippers to swim and walk.

herd—a group of the same kind of animals that live together

mammal—a warm-blooded animal that breathes air; mammals have hair or fur; female mammals feed milk to their young.

shellfish—an animal protected by a shell; clams, oysters, and crabs are shellfish.

tusk—a long front tooth; walruses use their tusks for fighting and getting out of the water; walruses have 18 teeth, but only two are tusks.

whisker—a long hair near the mouth of an animal; walruses have 400 to 700 whiskers.

Read More

Miller, Connie Colwell. *Walruses.* World of Mammals. Mankato, Minn.: Capstone Press, 2006.

Murray, Julie. *Walruses.* A Buddy Book. Edina, Minn.: Abdo, 2003.

Rustad, Martha E. H. *Walruses.* Ocean Life. Mankato, Minn.: Capstone Press, 2003.

Internet Sites

FactHound offers a safe, fun way to find Internet sites related to this book. All of the sites on FactHound have been researched by our staff.

Here's how:

1. Visit *www.facthound.com*

2. Choose your grade level.

3. Type in this book ID **0736867260** for age-appropriate sites. You may also browse subjects by clicking on letters, or by clicking on pictures and words.

4. Click on the **Fetch It** button.

FactHound will fetch the best sites for you!

Index

Word Count: 117
Grade: 1
Early-Intervention Level: 14